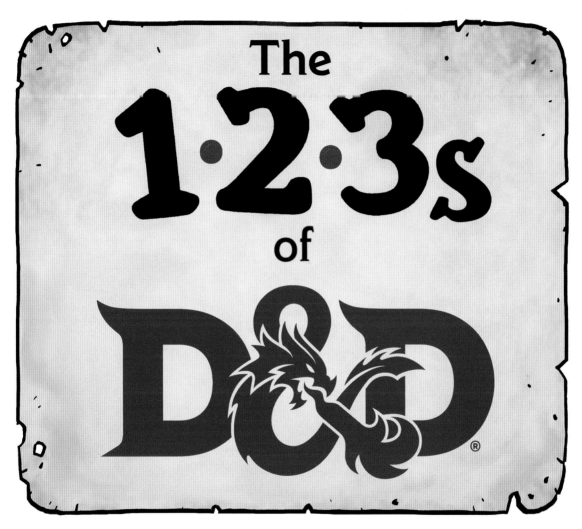

The 1·2·3s of D&D

Written by Ivan Van Norman
Illustrated by Caleb Cleveland

We begin with **ONE** Dungeon Master telling a story of daring deeds,

... the adventure of TWO heroes and
their brave and noble steeds.

They battle against THREE goblins,
snarling and mean,

... to find and save **FOUR** travelers
in a very exciting scene.

The heroes visit FIVE towers,
a city on the boom,

... to hear the words of SIX scholars, with a prophecy of doom:

But beware of EIGHT liches,
who guard them from the brash."

With the help of NINE dragons,
the heroes will save the day.

But when the clock strikes TEN,
it's time to hit the hay!

BESTIARY

ALHOONS prefer to dine on brains and cackle in their caves.

The ALMIRAJ are tiny, but their little hearts are brave.

An **AXE BEAK** is a trusty mount, but it's hard to ride.

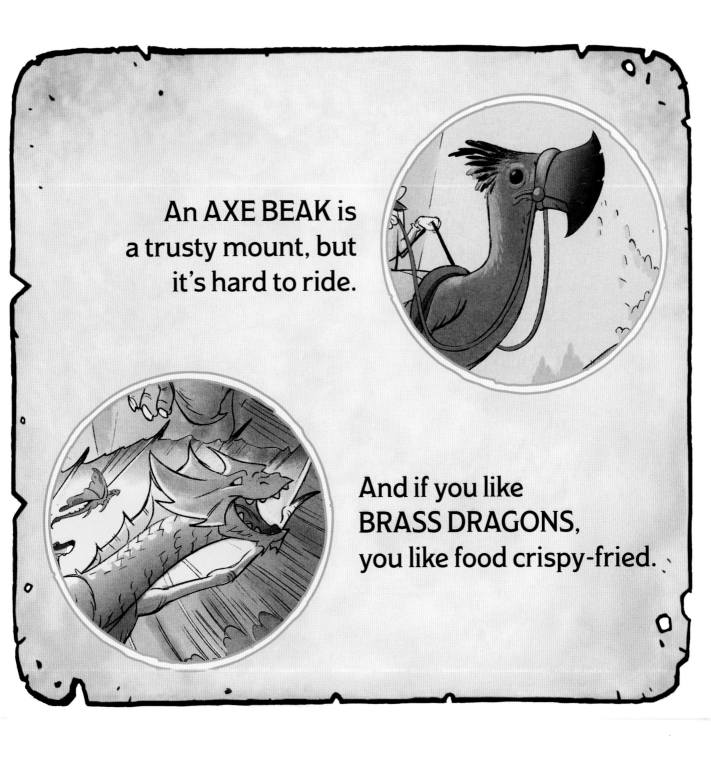

And if you like **BRASS DRAGONS**, you like food crispy-fried.

And then there are BRONZE DRAGONS, who like the beach and sea.

But make sure you never bring a BUGBEAR home for tea.

A COPPER DRAGON
can tell some funny tales.

But the DROW
are grumpy and live
underground with snails.

Every haunted house has a GHOST or two.

But if you want to party, then GOBLINS are for you!

If it's wisdom that you're seeking, then GOLD DRAGONS are the best.

But if you seek a HOBGOBLIN, then fighting is your quest.

A LICH is evil, and its heart is filled with ire.

RED DRAGONS sit on piles of gold and toast you with their fire.

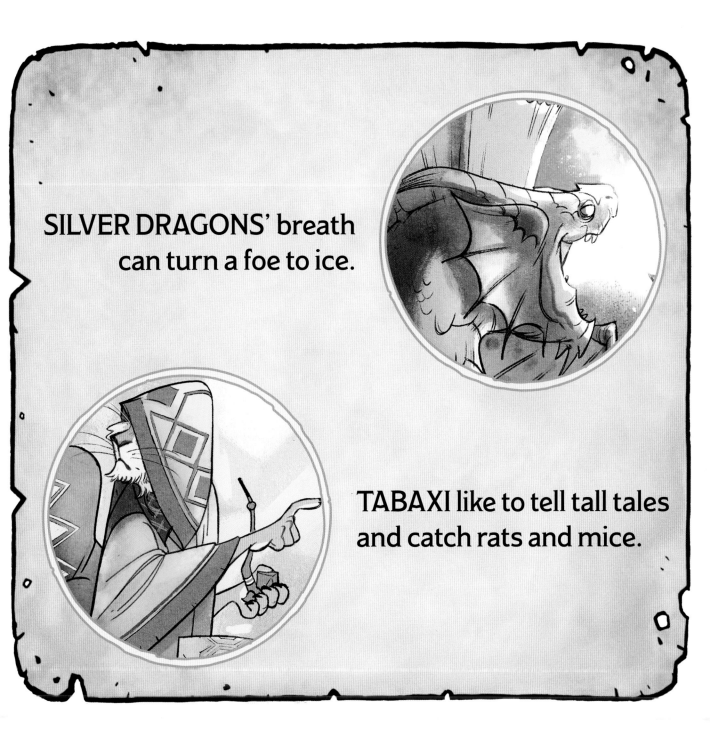

SILVER DRAGONS' breath
can turn a foe to ice.

TABAXI like to tell tall tales
and catch rats and mice.

The UNICORN is mystical, with a magic horn that can heal.

And then there are WHITE DRAGONS, which will lie and cheat and steal.

All these monsters you can meet
When playing D&D.
So have fun on your adventures,
And save a spot for me!

Writing: Ivan Van Norman
Art: Caleb Cleveland
Layout: Christopher J. De La Rosa
Additional Writing: Michele Carter, Adam Lee
Art Direction: Kate Irwin
Managing Editor: Jeremy Crawford

620C6118001001 EN
ISBN: 978-0-7869-6668-4
First Printing: August 2018

9 8 7 6 5 4 3

Printed in China. ©2020 Wizards of the Coast LLC, PO Box 707, Renton, WA 98057-0707, USA. Manufactured by: Hasbro SA, Rue Emile-Boéchat 31, 2800 Delémont, CH. Represented by: Hasbro, De Entree 240, 1101 EE Amsterdam, NL. Hasbro UK Ltd., PO Box 43 Newport, NP19 4YH, UK.

dungeonsanddragons.com